Real Dramas by Fred M White

Fred Merrick White was born in 1859 in West Bromwich in the Midlands of England to Joseph White and Helen Merrick who had married the previous year.

Joseph was a solicitor's managing clerk, who by the time the family moved to Hereford a few years later, had become a solicitor's article clerk.

Little is known of White's early years but what is known is that he followed in his father's footsteps and worked as a solicitor's clerk in Hereford. His father by now had also become a solicitor and times seemed quite prosperous for the family.

However in the late 1880's something went badly wrong for his father and he was imprisoned.

White had by now decided that writing was a more preferable career for him than the law. By 1891 Fred M. White, now 31 years old, was working full-time as a journalist and author, earning enough to support himself and his mother, Helen. By this time Fred's younger brother, Joseph A. White, had left home and working as a glass-blower.

In 1892, White married Clara Jane Smith. The wedding took place at King's Norton, Worcestershire, and the couple went on to have two children; Sydney Eric White (1893) and Ormond John White (1895).

As the century closed Fred's father had been released from prison and was living as a "retired solicitor", together with Helen, in Worthington in West Sussex.

By the time of the 1911 census, Fred M. White, now 52 years old, and his wife Clara were living at Uckfield, a town in the Wealden district of East Sussex. As the ominous shadows of the First World War gathered White had established himself as a popular and extremely prolific author. Indeed whether it was novels or short stories they flowed from his pen with a startling speed and many of them were initially serialized in the popular weekly and monthly magazines. His clever use of science to create imaginative and highly adventurous story lines was a particular talent of his.

During the First World War, both of his sons served as junior officers in The Royal Inniskilling Fusiliers.

The titanic struggle of the First World War and his sons' war-time experiences in it greatly influenced this phase of his writing. His novel The Seed of Empire (1916), describes early trench warfare in great and gritty detail. He went on to describe how the social changes after the war created many problems for returning soldiers as they attempted to fit back into a now peaceful society.

Fred and Clara spent their twilight years in Barnstaple in Devon, an area which also provided the backdrop for his novels The Mystery Of Crocksands, The Riddle Of The Rail, and The Shadow Of The Dead Hand.

Fred Merrick White died in Barnstaple in 1935.

Index of Contents

CHAPTER I

HIS SECOND SELF

The hard faced man with the thin, straggling beard and shaven upper lip glanced about him with a certain sour contempt. He had no approval for this frivolity. He lived by time and rule himself—he was partially shaven because his father and grandfather had been so before him; he wore an old fashioned pepper and salt suit for the same reason. So long as he could remember, he had dined every Sunday at one o'clock on cold beef and a cold suet pudding. He had lived in the same house for sixty years with the same polished mahogany, the same hard, strong horsehair chairs, waited on practically by the same sour, hard servants. Year in and year out, he had travelled the same round to the same dingy office where he made the same money almost to a penny, keeping to the same faiths and prejudices. The dreary monotony of it had killed his wife, and with her the one touch of romance in his grey existence; it had driven his only daughter away (to his great anger and indignation), for he regarded his house off Keppel Street as the acme of luxury and refinement.

In his way, Samuel Burton was a type. It is a type happily getting rare now, but he was an individuality all the same. The man was rigidly just and fair according to his lights, cold and unfeeling and ready always to justify some hard deed with appropriate extracts from Holy Writ. That he was lonely and unhappy and miserable he did not dream. The knowledge would have astonished him. That there was a deep humanity under his hard grey exterior would have astonished him still more.

He had not gone deliberately to the charitable entertainment given by the Bloomsbury Thespian Society—he had been more or less drawn there by false pretences. By mistake he had found himself in the lesser hall instead of the greater one, and, having paid his half crown, decided, in his characteristic way, to get the full benefit of it. A pretty girl dressed as a theatre attendant thrust a programme into his hand. He smiled sourly as he read it.

He had not been to a frivolous gathering like this for five and twenty years. For one brief month in the long ago he had tasted of these insidious joys. There were many reasons why he did not care to think of that period now. Had he kept clear of that, he would never have married, he would never have had a daughter to leave him in his old age. There was another side to the model, but Samuel Burton never glanced at that. To do so was to doubt his own judgment.

The first item on the programme was a three part comedy. It was a light and amusing little piece, and it pleased the audience immensely. Burton sat it out without the moving of a muscle. It seemed odd that people should laugh at that kind of thing. It wasn't a bit like life either. No woman would be such a fool as to cry because her young husband had pretended to forget her birthday. Everything in the little comedy depended on that. It seemed silly to Burton; it seemed absurd that a pleasant looking girl by him should wipe her eyes as the curtain came down. Burton had no idea that he was watching a dainty little masterpiece of French comedy, written by a master of his craft, skilled in the art of blending laughter and tears. He could not recognise the human document. It was impossible for him to know that the people round him were feeling all the better for it. It was all a silly waste of time and money.

A few songs and sketches followed. Then the stage manager came forward and made an announcement. He much regretted the impossibility of producing 'A Novel Engagement,' as promised by the programme. Miss Vavasour, of the Comus Theatre, who had engaged to play the leading part, was too ill to appear. She had very kindly arranged for the void to be filled by sending at her own expense Mr. Vincent Brook and Miss Elsie Montgomery (his wife) and their child, in a sketch of their own, called 'We Two.' The performers were new to London audiences, but they had played with considerable success in the provinces, and Miss Vavasour hoped that the audience would feel that she had done rather better for them than would have been the case had she been in a condition to appear personally. The audience applauded charitably.

Samuel Burton had half a mind to get up and go out. He was rather inclined to be angry with himself for staying so long. He would have scornfully rejected the suggestion that he was interested—that, on the whole, he had enjoyed the last sketch. He was just a little startled on glancing down his programme to see that the name of the lady in 'We Two' was Elsie Montgomery. That had been the name of his wife before her marriage. He recollected how his father used to scoff at her. The old man had always regarded her as a poor, frivolous creature. But the frivolity had not lasted long. A sensitive plant of that kind does not flourish in the atmosphere of horsehair chairs.

It was no more than a coincidence, of course. Burton had noticed that the theatrical people were fond of names full flavoured and high sounding. Still, he would just stay and see what this 'Elsie Montgomery' was like. The curtain went up presently on a dismal looking low sitting room in a lodging house. A pale, slender, pretty woman in rusty black was arranging a few faded flowers in a jug. She hummed a gay air to herself as she stood back and contemplated her handiwork. The air ended on a jarring note, the tears came into her eyes. She dropped into a broken chair by the side of a deal table and covered her face with her hands. A burst of sobbing came from her heart. A thrill ran through the audience. Here was the real thing, the striking of the true pathetic note. Burton was stirred, in spite of himself. What was the matter with the woman?

She looked up again and dashed the tears from her eyes. The white face was full of defiance. Burton leant forward and grasped the arm of his chair tightly. He was looking into the face of the dead and gone Elsie Montgomery. He had seen his wife look just like that more than once. It had been her way when he had denied her some little harmless pleasure, some break in the monotony of her drab existence. Surely, imagination was playing tricks with him. It was no more than a chance likeness.

"If I felt certain," the woman said, "I would leave him to night. But how do I know?"

Elsie's voice! Elsie's voice, beyond the shadow of a doubt. What was the meaning of it? Then gradually it all became plain to Samuel Burton. He was watching his own daughter. It was unkind of fate to play this shabby trick upon him. For five and twenty years he had not been in a place like this, and yet the very first time after so long an interval......

Somebody was asking him to sit down. He realised suddenly that he had risen to his feet. As he dropped into his seat again his face flushed. He took a grip of himself. Really, it was nothing more than a coincidence. His daughter had deliberately chosen her own way, and she must take the consequences of her act. She had married a shabby vagabond with her eyes open. She had foolishly supposed that the man she married had had the making of a great painter in him. There was money in art, of course, but not for Vincent Brook. He was still in the depths or obscurity.

Burton did not call this acting at all. It was probably the real thing. Doubtless this was the kind of house that Elsie had grown accustomed to. She looked as if she was frequently hard pressed to get a meal. A little child of theirs, a tiny tot of a girl, came into the room. She was dressed in white, daintily and elegantly dressed, in painful contrast to the mother. Burton stirred again uneasily. This was his grandchild, he could remember Elsie something like that when she was a child, and she had stood at his knees and played with his watch chain.... What was the matter with his spectacles?

"Real good stuff, isn't it?" a man by Burton's side murmured to his neighbour. "Really kind of Kitty Vavasour to stand down and give 'em a chance. Pity to see talent starving."

"Is it as bad as that?" the other man asked. "But what's the matter with Brook's painting?"

"Didn't you hear? Why, you haven't been to the Savage much lately. Poor beggar had trouble with his eyes. Just as he was getting on nicely, too. Doctor absolutely forbade him to touch a pencil for three years. Said he'd be all right at the end of that time. They had to do something, so they put up this sketch between them. Yes, the child is their own. They tell me she has a cold hearted old brute of a father somewhere—sort of chap who lives for money. He turned her out when she married Brook, and as I told you before, they have been starving ever since. Kitty Vavasour got them this chance. Pretended that she was ill and couldn't turn up tonight."

In an odd kind of way, Burton found himself echoing the speaker's sentiment. It seemed to him that he was somebody else seated in judgment on Samuel Burton's conduct. No doubt the man was a hard, cold, close fisted individual. He had behaved exceedingly badly to his only child, whose one sin was that she married for love. He could see quite plainly now why Brook had not been successful. He was following the little play with careful attention. He even saw the drift of it before it was entirely plain to the rest of the audience, The half blind Brooks was still deeply in love with his wife. He blamed himself deeply for bringing her to her present state of poverty and suffering. He did not say as much, but he showed by a score of little acts. At the same time he was cold and almost brutal in his manner, as if he were trying to force a quarrel on his wife. His idea was to make her leave him and go back to her own people. If he could kill her love for him, then his path in the future would be so much easier. Surely the audience were very stupid not to see this. Burton began to have quite a contempt for them. If folks had not a nice appreciation of these fine points, why then did they come to the theatre at all?

In a dim kind of way the heroine grasped what was passing in her husband's mind. The little child held them together by a silken thread; it was on the babyish things prattled by her at the moment of crisis that the situation became plain. Burton followed it all with an interest that was alert and painful. He sat there learning a lesson. Nothing of the kind had come into his life before. Of the nobility of sacrifice he had known nil. He seemed to see himself stripped of his garb of sham humanity, to be wandering through a crowd of angry eyes, naked and ashamed. He saw himself upon the stage—the figure of the stern father made up more or less in his own likeness coming there to take his daughter back again. The audience hissed vigorously. And Burton found himself hissing there with a zest that was all his own. Something was the matter with his spectacles again. He saw the stage through a mist.

"A fine bit of realistic acting, Sir," his neighbour said.

Burton had nothing by way of reply. It was no acting so far as he was concerned. In a few brief moments he was learning the lesson of a lifetime. It was such love as this that Elsie Montgomery had brought to him. And he had coldly and deliberately turned his back upon it. And he had expected Elsie Montgomery's daughter to sit down to the drab atmosphere of Keppel Street and eventually marry a grey counterpart of himself, who only differed from him in the measure of his years! He thought of the horsehair chairs and the polished mahogany table and hated them with a whole hearted intensity.

The fall of the curtain disturbed him. There was no tragedy. A timely bit of luck gave to the husband the independence that he craved for. It inclined him to throw off the mask and confess what he had done and why—it enabled him to refuse the suggestion of the father and show him the door with a passion that was slightly in the nature of an anticlimax, but apparently human enough to move the audience to a burst of enthusiastic applause....

Burton stumbled into the street. The touch of cold air on his face, the passing of feet brought him to his senses again. In that brief half hour he had learned his lesson. But the facts remained. The time might come when Elsie and her child would be independent of him, but that was not yet. In the meantime they were starving. He would follow them.

"Would you kindly tell me what this means, Sir?" Brook asked coldly.

Burton put his hands as if to ward off a blow.

"I have come to make peace," he said. "I have come to ask you to forgive me. An hour ago I was a hard, practical business machine; now I am a lonely old man who realises that he has ruined his life by his own want of charity. By accident I saw your little play to night. By accident there came to me the lesson that I needed. I poisoned existence for my wife; I did my best for my daughter in the same direction. And, honestly, I thought that I was doing the right thing. I sat in that hall to night and joined the audience in hissing and hooting at myself. This is a hard confession for a man of my age to make, but it has to be done."

Elsie Brook rose to her feet and glanced timidly at her husband. He made no sign. Burton could read what was passing through his mind.

"I can understand," he said. "I dare say that I should feel as you do. But I want to help you if I can. I want to prove to you that your drawing of the father's character is all wrong. And I want the child to stand at my knees as Elsie used to do. I'll promise you that she shall find me a different man to the father Elsie remembers. Let us make the story complete, Brook—let us give it a happy ending. And you shall go away and nurse your eyesight, you shall have the best advice that money can buy, you shall make a name and fame for yourself, my boy. And if anybody tells me again that there is no moral lesson to be gained in the theatre, why—"

"Sit down and have some supper," Brook said drily.

"Let's go out and buy it," Burton said unsteadily. "And after to night—well, well, I won't make any boast, but you shall see for yourselves that the world is worth living in, after all!"

CHAPTER II

AN "EXTRA TURN"

The true story of Audrey Marbowe's dramatic appearance on the variety stage and her subsequent phenomenal success has never been told before so far as the pages of a newspaper are concerned. Giles Gilman gives the facts occasionally, but only to those that he can trust, and even then he has to be in one of his pessimistic moods, when things are going badly and there is no gratitude in the world. As all those whose business is connected with theatrical matters know, Giles Gilman is the Napoleon of Press agents. More than one famous actress of to day would still be struggling for recognition had it not been for the happy inventiveness of Giles Gilman. Given a certain amount of brains and beauty, Gilman's clients were seldom failures. His ingenious inventiveness did the rest.

Two years ago Audrey Marbowe had not been heard of in England—that is, so far as the stage is concerned. To day she can command a salary of four hundred pounds a week in London, and more when she goes on a trip to her home in the United States. In New York society, however, she had been a familiar figure as the only daughter of Cyrus P. Marbowe, the Quinine King, and reported to be one of the richest men in America. He possessed a palace on Fifth Avenue, a cottage at Newport, a few lines of railway, and other necessities of the Transatlantic millionaire. It was said that on his daughter's marriage he was prepared to dower her to the extent of twenty million dollars. As she was young and pretty and highly educated, her value in the marriage market stood high. She had refused an English duke, and a German Prince had gone sorrowfully and empty away.

Audrey Marbowe had always been a girl of moods. She was volatile and changeable, but there was one ambition of hers that always glowed clearly and steadily. Her great desire was to be an actress. She possessed histrionic talents beyond doubt; she was the bright star of a fashionable amateur club; the newspapers said pretty things about her. But Audrey was not unduly puffed up by these. She quite understood why the daughter of a millionaire had the primrose path swept and garnished for her. She wanted to appear on the regular stage and make a name for herself. But here Cyrus P. was adamant. Any other extravagant folly he was prepared to pay for. He drew the line at the stage. He had on one occasion speculated in theatres, and, in his own parlance, he knew something.

But when a pretty girl with the command of money sets her heart on a thing, Fate generally conspires to meet her halfway. Fate in this case took the shape of a shrewd, well dressed, keen eyed individual, who was known in dramatic circles as Giles Gilman. Amongst other extravagances, Audrey had a little 'bachelor' flat, and there she invited Gilman to tea. She knew beforehand that she was entertaining the most astute Press agent in America.

"Now I want you to help me," she said; "I told you all about myself last night. And you have already seen me in several parts. Will I do?"

"There have been many big reputations built up on a more slender basis," Gilman replied. "There is not the slightest reason why you should not succeed. It will cost money, of course. Personally, I should advise you to go on as you are. And if your father interferes—"

"He's not going to interfere," Audrey smiled. "I guess that the parental battery is spiked. I hope that you can keep a secret, Mr. Gilman."

Gilman protested, with justice, that he was the soul of discretion. Audrey lent towards him and whispered a few words that caused even the imperturbable agent to look surprised.

"That is about the last thing I should have thought of," he said. "Still, from a business point of view, it simplifies matters exceedingly. You would like to appear in London, of course. Say the Majestic. It would be to your advantage to start on the vaudeville stage. As Miss Marbowe in the famous pearls!"

Audrey Marbowe clasped her hands together. Here was fame indeed. And the little man with the alert eyes was promising it as if it had been the easiest matter in the world.

"I hope you are not making fun of me," she asked.

"My dear Madam," Gilman said gravely, "this is business. We stand here as client and agent. I get you this engagement, and you pay me so much money. All I want you to do is exactly what you are told, not forgetting the famous pearls. The 'story' is not yet complete, but I shall get it fixed up in a day or two, when I will write you fully and definitely. To try and get an engagement off hand at the Majestic would be a mere waste of time. Besides, I never ask favours. I prefer to confer them."

Gilman departed without saying any more, and for the next three weeks Audrey Marbowe saw him no more. Neither did he write her a line. But she noticed that the papers had a good deal to say about her famous pearls, round which something in the nature of a romance had been woven. They were just the kind of paragraphs that the exchanges were after.

At the same time, the Press had a certain amount to say as to one Lola Cortez, a Spanish American, who seemed to be making a considerable name for herself in San Francisco. A week ago nobody had heard of her. Now she began to be talked about everywhere. She appeared to be one of those fortunate persons who 'arrive' in the course of a single night. It would be an interesting study to work up the psychology of these artistic and literary cuckoos.

There were alert managers on the lookout for new talent who would write to California asking questions and suggesting terms. But, apparently, they were too late. It was understood that Lola Cortez had accepted an engagement to appear in London in two months' time. Audrey Marbowe read all this with a certain interested jealousy. How lucky some people were, and how easily they seemed to get their chance! She was still speculating over this philosophy when a bulky letter from Gilman reached her. She was urged to read it again and again, until she had it practically by heart. After that, she was to destroy the letter, and do just as she was told therein.

Two days later the New York papers came out scarred and striped with scare heads. Old man Marbowe had gone down. There had been a sharp financial crisis, and the house of Marbowe had gone under. The Quinine King, instead of being worth millions, was worth nothing. On the contrary, there was a deficit of many millions. The air was heavy with sinister rumours. Marbowe would be lucky if he escaped an indictment for forgery and fraud. He was at present lying on a sick bed in a state of utter prostration.

All this appeared in double columns.

In parallel double columns, Miss Audrey Marbowe figured with equal prominence. She had for ever turned her back on the delights and frivolities of society for the fascinations of the stage. That would be definitely her career in the future, She was on the eve of sailing in the 'Pacific' for England to fulfill an engagement at a leading theatre. The fact that Signora Lola Cortez was travelling to Europe on the same boat was merely mentioned in a curt paragraph on the leader page. It was rather hard upon Miss Cortez, but circumstances were against her. As her Press agent, Giles Gilman openly deplored the fact.

He stepped on board the 'Pacific' with the object of offering a few well chosen words of condolence to Miss Marbowe. She came forward, her grief chastened by a certain joy, a bundle of papers under her arm. There was a gleam in her eye that Gilman did not fail to notice.

"Say, isn't it fine?" she whispered. "I guess you understand how to work things. Miss Cortez—"

Gilman was going to say good bye to Miss Cortez also. She had gone down to her cabin a little time before. But Miss Cortez took so much finding that Gilman found himself the victim of a great annoyance. The 'Pacific' started whilst he was still aboard. Much against his will, he was destined to remain where he was until the boat reached Liverpool. No doubt he could manage to borrow a wardrobe, and assuredly he was very fortunate in that direction. He turned out so smartly and so immaculately that he might have had a portmanteau smuggled on board. One never can tell.

It was next day that the tragic discovery was made. Miss Marbowe was nowhere to be found! The boat was ransacked from one end to the other; the painful tragedy ran from lip to lip. And nobody could throw any light on the mystery. Miss Marbowe had come on board without a maid; she had engaged one to meet her in Liverpool. She had not appeared at dinner the first night, alleging that the motion of the boat had given her a headache. As she did not show up at breakfast, the door of her cabin was forced and found to be empty! Long before the boat reached Liverpool the distressing story of Miss Marbowe's suicide was told by Marconi gram. On the arrival of the 'Pacific', the passengers were confronted with the whole story.

In a sorrowful frame of mind, Gilman accompanied his second client to London. Now that the bright particular star had fallen from the sky, he was fain to be content with the minor planet. He would do great things for her, of course, but nothing like he had anticipated in the case of Miss Marbowe.

The management of the Majestic had not been idle. They were prepared to give Miss Cortez a good run for her money, and they had billed her extensively. She appeared in due course, and, on the whole, had no occasion to be disappointed with her reception. According to the papers, she was an actress of far more than the average merit. Her dresses were exquisite and jewels superb. The lady writers were quite enthusiastic over her pearls.

A moment later the manager, pale and agitated, came forward to explain. "A most unfortunate thing has happened," he said. "An extraordinary mistake on the fart of the police. They allege that Signora Cortez's pearls are actually the property of the late Miss Marbowe, the famous American beauty who disappeared from the 'Pacific' some days ago."

The people at the Majestic were perfectly satisfied. A great house had gathered on the third night to see the new 'star' from South America. Miss Cortez had sung her first song and had come forward with the intention of giving an encore, when she was suddenly drawn aside and the curtain fell. London audiences are not accustomed to be treated in this fashion, and they signified their disapproval vigorously. A moment later the manager, pale and agitated, came forward to explain.

"A most unfortunate thing has happened," he said. "An extraordinary mistake on the part of the police. They allege that Signora Cortez's pearls are actually the property of the late Miss Marbowe, the famous American beauty who disappeared from the 'Pacific' some days ago. The Signora is accused stealing the pearls, if nothing worse. The thing is a hideous blunder, of course, but in the circumstances, ladies and gentlemen; you will see why Signora Cortez cannot sing again to night. I am quite sanguine that she will appear before you again to morrow."

Here was a sensation the like of which the theatrical world had never seen before. The morning papers were devoted to very little else. The afternoon edition came out with fresh details with nothing in them. The Signora had been charged at Bow Street, and finally remanded on bail. The next day the 'Daily Mail' had solved the problem. Possibly, a long interview with Giles Gilman, and the interchange of a pink slip of paper, had something to do with it.

It really was an astounding story. To begin with, the lady known as Lola Cortez had been charged with stealing her own properly. As a matter of fact, there was no such person as the Cortez. She had existed merely in the imagination of the agent who was acting Miss Marbowe. The paragraphs from San Francisco were mere fakes, invented so as to get at the management of the Majestic. Directly the engagement had been entered into Lola Cortez vanished into the air. Somebody in her name had taken a cabin in the 'Majestic' and some luggage followed. Miss Marbowe had not vanished overboard—she had simply disguised herself and taken possession of Lola Cortez's cabin. From that moment she was Lola Cortez, and Miss Marbowe ceased to exist. She had done this partly to get her on the London stage, and partly because she found that at the last moment her father's creditors might seize the pearls. She had always intended, of course, to disclose her real identity after her reputation was made. Where she had made the mistake, of course, was to wear her pearls.

The effect of all this can easily be imagined. The 'Majestic' was packed from floor to ceiling for weeks afterwards, and Miss Marbowe, nee Cortez, was earning her own salary. In any case she was worth her money, for there was no question as to her abilities and talent. At the same time there was no disguising the fact that luck was all on her side. Undoubtedly she was born to success, but in ordinary circumstances she would never have found herself at the outset on the crest of a wave. On the whole, she accepted the situation with modesty and humour. But she would have nothing further to do with Gilman. He had been paid handsomely, and there was an end of the matter. It was this base ingratitude that caused him to tell the story to discreet ears in moments of expansion.

"Of course, I worked the whole thing," he was wont to explain. "Directly she told me that her father was on the verge of a smash I began to see my way. I invented Lola Cortez, and got all those pars in the papers about her. Then I settled the other details after I managed to get 'Lola' on the 'Majestic.' It was easy for her to slip away in the confusion of sailing. Everything was ready for Audrey Marbowe there. She had only to change cabins and disguise herself—it was especially simple as nobody on the boat knew either of them. The real touch of genius came in over the pearls. It was I who dropped an anonymous letter to the police over the pearls, and I laid my plans to get the arrest made at the proper dramatic moment. The father's creditors business was all bosh. And naturally the manager of the 'Majestic' saw his chance. And I'm bound to say that he was not ungrateful. The story slipped out so naturally that the English public never saw that it had been gulled. Everybody wanted to see Audrey Marbowe, and she, to do her justice, was quite equal to the occasion. If she hadn't got the right stuff in her I should never have taken a hand. I've done very well out of it, but hang it, I hate ingratitude and I told her so. And now there is nothing more for me than a cold bow when we meet. Says it is necessary to be discreet."

"She'll marry you in the end, my boy," one of the listeners said prophetically. "When women treat a man like that they always end by marrying him."

Gilman shook his head as he took a fresh cigarette.

"I shall never marry," he said firmly. "I shall never play the game again. If I did so there is a little girl in a company up North that fairly—what are you fellows laughing at now?"

CHAPTER III

"NOT IN THE BILL"

When young Lord Strandford came or age there were festivities in honour of the occasion at Strandford Park, the family seat in Loamshire. As everybody knows, the Mepherhams are an extremely good old family, somewhat simple and unaffected, and by no means meriting the title of 'up to date.' As a matter of fact they would have resented anything of the kind as suggestive of the modern financier of Teutonic origin, the like of which would have had a poor chance of obtaining admission beyond the gates of Strandford Park—unless they came on Mondays and Fridays to see the pictures.

Therefore it was considered a daring innovation on Lady Challenger's part when she suggested theatricals. An amateur performance was not in her mind at all—greatly daring, she wanted to have a professional company, and a drama performed by them in the Rubens Gallery.

Lord Challenger raised no objection, provided that the expense was not too great. Dramatic 'stars,' of course, were out of the question. How to set about it was hardly less difficult a matter. Almost in despair, Lady Challenger wrote to a friend who had a position almost unique as a leading amateur. Really the thing was quite simple, the reply came. Lady Challenger had only to state her requirements in a letter to Blank's Dramatic Agency, 1194, Strand, and the thing was done. She would be able to pick her own play, and, as Strandford Park was on a main line, the whole company could catch the down express and be back in London by half past one. All trains could be stopped by signal at Strandford Park Station. The rest was merely the signing of the necessary cheque.

Really it was delightfully simple. Messrs. Blank were quite willing to supply a competent cast, they had the honour of submitting some comedy dramas for her Ladyship's selection. The fee would be so much, and Messrs. Blank would produce the play, erect the stage, and generally manage the proceedings.

Like most simple minded ladies who pass most of their time in the country, Lady Challenger was of a romantic turn. She wanted a pretty play with considerable emotion in it. She finally made selection of a piece founded on an incident in one of Wilkie Collins' novels—the story of a persecuted woman who suffered punishment for the crime of another. It really was a pretty story, and Lady Challenger shed tears over the woes of Hester Walters, the innocent convict.

She was interested in women convicts, and, indeed, she knew something of their habits. The female prison at Oldchester was only four miles away, and Lady Challenger was one of the visitors. No doubt this fact influenced her in choosing the play.

Messrs. Blank's representatives duly appeared, a pretty little stage was elected in the Rubens Gallery, the invitations were out, and the programme printed. The dramatic performance was the culminating point in a long day's festivities. There was a cricket match against the Free Foresters in the Park, a dinner for the workmen on the estate at mid day, and a children's fete in the afternoon. The house was filled to its utmost capacity. At four o'clock most of the talented cast arrived, and immediately proceeded to dine. Lady Challenger was pleased to be present.

"I hope you have a good company, Mr. Trenor?" said her Ladyship.

"I can confidently say so, Lady Challenger," Mr. Vernon Trenor, the stage manager smiled. "To all practical purposes we have a London company. We are all artists. Most of us are under contract to the big managers—we accept these engagements by special arrangement."

Lady Challenger smilingly accepted the assurance. Everything appeared to be going very smoothly indeed. And really these good people looked very nice, quite presentable. It was astonishing what a lot of well bred people took to the stage nowadays! Still, Lady Challenger was just a little displeased. She had particularly desired a few words with 'Hester Walters,' and that heroine not yet arrived.

"She could not possibly come down with the rest of us," the manager explained. "She has a sick relative with whom she desired to stay until the last moment. We brought her dresses with us and she will be here herself by the 7.46, which stops here. She knows that it is only a few minutes' walk across the park. I am sorry that your Ladyship should be disappointed."

"You see I am acquainted with real convicts," Lady Challenger smiled. "I am a frequent visitor at Oldchester Prison. Some most interesting cases there, I assure you. Not real criminals, but poor creatures unable to resist a sudden temptation."

"Wasn't there an accident at Oldchester last night?" Trenor asked.

"Oh, yes; might have been very serious indeed, Mr. Trenor. An escape of gas and an explosion that wrecked part of the building. Happily, no lives were lost, though some of the creatures were badly hurt. I'm told that they are in a sad state of confusion."

Lady Challenger tripped away, having seen that her guests were made free of the house. She was pleased to find that they afforded quite an attraction in themselves. There were young people present who were glad of the chance of talking to real actors and actresses. They spread over the lovely old grounds, they explored the woods and shrubberies, relating their experiences to knots of appreciative listeners.

Trenor stared at her with open mouthed amazement. "But I don't understand," he stammered, "You are Miss Hillhouse at all."

As the hour for the performance drew near Mr. Trenor began to feel anxious. It was a little past the time now and Miss Hillhouse, who was down to play 'Hester Walters,' had not put in an appearance. If she had missed her train, then the performance would be spoilt. Fortunately, she did not come on till the middle of the first act, so that the curtain could go up without her. She came presently, in the nick of time, breathless and full of apologies. The train was late, she had missed the pathway in the gathering darkness, and had had a nasty fall over some brambles. She had managed to blunder into a boggy marsh, so that she was splashed and muddy. The long coat that hid her from head to foot was a mass of clay.

Trenor stared at her with open mouthed amazement.

"But, I don't understand," he stammered. "You are not Miss Hillhouse at all. In that case—"

"I quite forgot to explain," the newcomer gasped. "Miss Hillhouse could not come at the very last moment. She was detained, and telephoned to Messrs. Blank, who sent for me at once. Fortunately, I have played the part quite recently, so you need not be nervous on that score. Mr. Blank gave me my instructions, and I came as fast as I could. My name is Hill."

"Almost the same as Hillhouse," Trenor smiled. "I haven't had the pleasure of meeting you before."

"I am Australian," Miss Hill explained. "I have been touring in America and Africa. I only arrived in London a week ago. I suppose I shall be able to manage with my predecessors outfit and make up. I presume that it is here. Let me get to my dressing room at once. And could you procure me a few sandwiches and a glass of champagne? I missed my dinner to day, intending to dine late, and I had to come away without a meal at all."

Trenor was only too delighted. The anxiety was off his mind now, and everything was going smoothly. Miss Hill ate her sandwiches and drank her champagne with a fine healthy appetite. Trenor examined her make up with an approving eye. Miss Hillhouse's convict dress fitted her as if it had been made on purpose. There was no mistake about the strength and power of her performance either. Miss Hillhouse had been just a little too refined and ladylike for the part. The audience seemed to feel it too. They were quite carried away by the force and fire of the wronged heroine's acting. When the curtain fell on the first act there was a perfect hurricane of applause from the stalls and from the packed mass of farmers and tenantry behind. Lady Challenger came fussing into the dressing rooms in her kindly way, bent upon making the acquaintance of Miss Hill.

"We are charmed—delighted!" she said. "Really, you carried us right away. And I understand that you were so good as to come here at the very last moment. And you have had nothing since lunch but a few poor sandwiches and a glass of wine. Have you a long wait now?"

"Not more than half an hour," Miss Hill explained. "I don't have to change my dress at all."

"Capital!" Lady Challenger explained. "Then you will have time to get a proper meal. The house is more or less in a state of chaos, so I make no apology for asking you to have supper in my dressing room. I have had it set out for you there. I will take you there myself, and I will arrange for the call boy to fetch you directly you are required. Only you must not mind if I do not remain with you—I have so many little duties to attend to."

Miss Hill appeared to be overwhelmed by all this kindness. Indeed, it was a great deal more than she had any right to expect. And, after all, she was only doing what she was paid to do. Out in Australia and South Africa she had really known what hardships were. Nevertheless, she was quite ready to avail herself of this pleasing hospitality. She had a splendid appetite, and the sandwiches had not gone very far. One point she was firm upon—she was not going to trespass too far on Lady Challenger's good nature. She quite understood how busy the latter must be.

"Please do not consider me for a moment," she said. "I have given you too much trouble already. I shall not feel comfortable until you return to your guests, Lady Challenger. They will call me directly my presence is needed on the stage again. Please, please do not wait."

Lady Challenger took the speaker at her word. The performance went its smooth way until the final fall of the curtain and the inevitable triumph of virtue over vice. Then Miss Hill hurried upstairs, just as she was, to finish her supper, coming down finally to the dressing rooms after everybody had gone. She was some considerable time in removing her 'make up' and changing into everyday gait again. In this she good naturedly refused the services of a dresser.

"I am not going to keep you another moment," she said. "I should have come down before. Go away and get your supper with the rest of them. Tell Mr. Trenor that I shall not be more than half an hour at the outside. If only I had a clean pair of shoes—"

By this time the members of the theatrical company had mingled in the supper room with the rest of the guests. Lady Challenger was beginning to wonder what had become of Miss Hill. At the same moment the portly, dignified old butler approached Trenor with a certain suggestion of haste, and whispered something in his ear. The message appeared to be slightly incredible.

"The thing is impossible," he said. "It is a joke, a mistake on somebody's part."

"Perhaps it is, Sir," the butler said. "All the same, I shall be glad if you will come and see the young woman for yourself. She is very persistent in what she says, Sir."

Trenor hurried away into the morning room. There he found a somewhat dishevelled young lady, whose eyes were full of indignant tears. Her dress appeared to be considerably damaged.

"Miss Hillhouse!" Trenor gasped. "What is the meaning of this, please?"

"I only wish that I could tell you," the girl said faintly. "I was coming across the park to night when a woman encountered me. I stopped to speak to her and she promptly threw me down. She had a knife in her hand, and she threatened to kill me if I called out. She pushed my handkerchief in my mouth, and bound me fast with some rope that she had found somewhere. And there I lay, half dead, till some men found me and brought me here. They were poachers, I expect, for they did not stop. Then I rang the bell and saw the butler, and—well, here I am."

Tenor did some rapid thinking in the next few moments. In the first place, he desired to see Miss Hill without the lease delay. Miss Hill, strange to say, had left the house. She had gone away without the formality of saying good bye, she had helped herself to certain choice articles from Lady Challenger's wardrobe, including a complete outfit of lingerie and shoes. It was some little time before Lady Challenger could understand the real state of affairs. But it began to come home to her presently, after a brief but painful interview with her maid. Not only was Miss Hill and a portion of her wardrobe missing, but a valuable selection of jewels could not be found. They had gone also.

"But how was it managed?" the bewildered hostess asked. "How did she know, and how did she—"

"May I make a suggestion?" Trenor asked. "I have an idea. It is just possible that, during the confusion following the explosion at Oldchester Prison, one or more of the convicts escaped. The fact might have only just been found out. If Lord Challenger will telephone to the prison he may find that my surmise is correct. Evidently the escaped convict is an actress. She was probably hiding in the grounds to day, and heard all that she needed to know. A chance conversation gave her the idea. She wanted a change of garments and a good meal. There was a certain amount of risk in the whole business, but it was worth taking. The part of Hester Walters is one familiar to most emotional actresses who travel with stock companies. Really, it was quite easy."

Lord Challenger returned to the library presently with a grave face.

"Mr. Trenor is quite right," he explained. "I got the Governor of the prison on the telephone. It appears that two of the women are missing. One is Louisa Reynards, an Australian who has had a deal of experience on the stage. After hearing this I had the dressing room searched, and surely enough I found the real convict garb worn by the impudent impostor. She actually came here in her convict dress, with Miss Hillhouse's cloak over it. But she cannot be far away."

"I expect she is," Trenor said. "A woman like that generally knows a thing or two. There are at least two score of motors in the stables belonging to your various guests. Miss Reynards either took one of these on her own hook, or she persuaded one of the drivers to take her, say, as far as Barham Junction, where she could easily get a train to town. Once there, it is pretty certain that she can find friends to help her, especially as she has jewels that she can turn into money. I only hope that your Lordship will not blame us for the disaster."

Lord Challenger was a just man, and he didn't. One of the cars was missing, to return at the end of an hour and a half with an explanation that fitted in with what Trenor had suggested. Lady Challenger listened ruefully; she had no hope of seeing the actress or the jewels again, and in this she was not destined to a pleasant surprise.

"It has been a successful day, all the same," she told her husband. "But I don't think I shall try theatricals in the future. They are a little too dramatic for my taste."

CHAPTER IV

THE PLAGIARIST

Willoughby Harcourt was holding forth in that silvery voice of his which had such a fascinating charm, especially where the women were concerned. His appearance was as picturesque as his career had been. Everybody who took the slightest interest in theatrical matters knew his story. His father had been an actor of repute in his day; he had been killed abroad in a duel arising out of a passionate love affair. His mother had been the beautiful, headstrong Lady Gertrude Maltravers, who had married Harcourt in the teeth of the most bitter opposition on the part of her family—only to find herself a widow two years later. At fifteen, Willoughby Harcourt had been left quite alone in the world to make his own way. He had graduated through a strolling theatrical company to a position as the finest romantic actor of his day. To all outward seeming he was prosperous enough; he had his own theatre, and more or less a hand in his own plays. There were certain people in the inner circle who said that Harcourt was no more than the paid servant of a syndicate, drawing a salary and percentage on the takings. And according to these quidnuncs there had been very little profit lately. There were others still less charitable who declared that Harcourt was a good bit of a scamp.

Despite all this, he was a popular figure everywhere. His keen, handsome, boyish face and white hair carried him swimmingly. To get his acceptance to a dinner invitation was regarded as a high compliment, and Lady Mannington seemed to appreciate the fact.

It was Sunday night and there were only half a dozen round the table, all told. The oval table was one mass of pink orchids and pink shaded lights. The dinner proceeded with that smooth elegance on which Lady Mannington prided herself. The coffee and cigarette stage had arrived. The hostess preferred to take this interval at the table, so incidentally did Willoughby Harcourt. He liked to lounge there and talk, he liked the artistic confusion of silver and red wine and the litter of fruit before him. It was the hour when he talked best.

He had the conversation pretty well to himself, as usual. He was more than usually interesting too, for he was talking of a new play produced for the first time the night before in Manchester. As this was Sunday, only the barest details had appeared in the Sunday paper. The listeners were following every detail eagerly, none more eagerly than Dorothy Nation.

As a matter of fact, she had no right there at all. She was by way of being Lady Mannington's secretary: she wrote her ladyship's letters and invitations, she played her accompaniments—for Lady Mannington was really musical and a composer of more than average merit. Somebody had fallen out at the very last minute, and Lady Mannington hated a blank at the dinner table. Half good naturedly, half imperiously, she had commanded her companion's attendance.

"Really a fine play, though perhaps I ought not to say it," Harcourt murmured. "Still, that was the opinion of Manchester last night."

"Who is the author?" somebody asked. "Is Eugene Malet an assumed name?"

"Or is it spell Willoughby Harcourt?" somebody else suggested.

Harcourt smiled in a distinctly non committal manner. He made no denial.

"I should prefer not to answer that question," he said. "For some occult reason, the British public looks with a cold eye upon actor managers who write plays. It is their firm belief that somebody else does the work. I am not saying that there is no foundation for this. No doubt, Mr. Eugene Malet will disclose himself at the proper time."

The diners glanced at one another significantly. No doubt existed in the mind of one of them. Willoughby Harcourt had added another laurel to his crown. It was very modest of him to speak like this. He went on now to discuss the plot of the play.

"I flatter myself that the theme is extremely original," he said. "It's no novelty to have two men in love with the same woman, but in this case the men are father and son. The father has all the money, of course. He is under fifty, and a lover that any girl might be proud of. His son is twenty six, and he is equally well endowed by Nature. He takes his father into his confidence, never dreaming for a moment what the latter's feelings are. Like most sons, he looks upon his father as a bit of a fogey. The father makes no kind of a struggle to control his feelings, and he deliberately sets out to conspire against the young man's happiness. Unless he does that he knows that he has no chance. He gets the girl's father in his power, and sends him, a fugitive from justice, to Australia. The girl's parent thinks that there is a warrant out for his apprehension, and so does the girl. The time comes when she can save her father, and give him back the good name (which, as a matter of fact, he has not lost), by going out to Australia. It is a case of 'twixt love and duty.' Finally, duty conquers, as the father of the hero means that it should. The girl's father has gone away in an assumed name, and letters from him fall into the hands of the hero that makes it seem as if the heroine has fled to join an earlier lover. Then the action of the play is removed to Australia—to Melbourne. There is a painful scene in which the heroine (who has learnt many things) sees her lover through an open window talking to a girl—"

The girl blushed deeply. Lady Mannington was regarding her with cold displeasure. "Really, I am very sorry," she said contritely. "I—I was carried away by the story. I must have read this much in one of the Sunday papers."

"The girl his a necklace in her hand," Dorothy Nation interrupted eagerly. "It is a necklace which at one time the hero had offered to—I beg your pardon."

The girl blushed deeply. Lady Mannington was regarding her with cold displeasure.

"Really, I am very sorry," she said contritely. "I—I was carried away by the story. I must have read this much in one of the Sunday papers."

"Did you?" Harcourt asked with his most fascinating smile. "I did not think that they had been quite so enterprising. I thought I had seen them all, too. It is very good of you to follow my little story so closely. What was I saving? Oh, the incident of the necklace...... When the hero's father dies, as he does after a brief but painful illness, the story of his perfidy come out. It is at this point that the real dramatic grip of the story begins from......"

But Dorothy Nation was no longer listening. Her thoughts were far enough away at that moment. There was another story being played here under the eyes of the actor manager, and he was taking a part in it, had he only known it. And the story was far more intensely human, had he but understood. Dorothy came to herself with a start; the outline of the play was finished; Lady Mannington and her guests were going further on. A quarter of an hour later and Dorothy had the house in Stratton Street practically to herself. There was small chance of Lady Mannington returning for the next hour or two. The girl moved impulsively towards the door.

"I'll do it," she exclaimed. "I'll go as far as the Barbarian Club and see Mark German—he is always there on Sunday nights. I'll get him to help me to find 'Eugene Malet.' There is just a chance that I may find my happiness yet. And to think that that man could be such a mean thief! With his reputation, too! Well, we shall see."

It was not so very late yet, so that Dorothy decided to walk as far as the Barbarian. She was fortunate enough to find the popular theatrical agent on the premises. He came to her at once. He was a pleasant looking man with a clear eye and a firm square jaw.

"Dorothy Nation!" he exclaimed. "What do you want at this time of night?"

"I came to ask you a great favour," the girl said. "I want you to help me for the sake of the old time when you and my father were friends. You always said you would. You are the one man in England who knows most of my story; I owe my present situation to you. You helped me when I came back to England from Australia broken hearted and penniless. You never told anybody else?"

"My dear child, what a question! As if I should betray your confidence in that way!"

"I know, I know. Pray forgive me. Do you know, I heard my story repeated almost word for word in Stratton Street to night. It came from the lips of Willoughby Harcourt. I was so startled and alarmed that I nearly betrayed myself. Fancy my having to sit there at dinner whilst Harcourt related the tale of Herbert Stirling and his father!"

"Do you mean to say that the man was talking at you?"

"Oh, no. He was repeating the plot of his play produced in Manchester last night. As you know, it is a new play written by a man who appears on the programme as Eugene Malet."

"Practically the same thing as if it were Harcourt's name. Go on."

"Mr. German, Willoughby Harcourt never wrote that play. He insinuated to night that he was the author of it, but he lied. The play is based entirely upon the vile conspiracy by which Herbert Stirling's father came between his son and myself, it is woven into the play—it is the play itself. And the only two living people who know that story to day are Herbert Stirling and myself. That Herbert would divulge the details to anybody else I decline to believe. At the present moment he is somewhere in the world looking for me; I should look for him, only I am a poor girl, and I have my living to get. I began to fear that Herbert was dead; but I know better now. He is not dead, because he is the man who wrote the play now being rehearsed at the Apollo, under the name of Eugene Malet. He always had an ambition that way, probably he has gone abroad again, having expressed his determination never to return to England. He sent the play to Willoughby Harcourt, and he liked it. He is going to tacitly accept the suggestion that he wrote it. With his reputation—"

"Yes, I know what you are going to say," German observed thoughtfully. "Harcourt's reputation is none too good amongst those of us who are behind the scenes. More than once he has had a play written to order that contained ideas from dramas forwarded to him by aspirants. I'll go and see him if you like, and try and get a general admission out of him. But I'm afraid that is not much use unless I have some facts to go upon. Something startling, I mean."

"Then I'll give them to you," Dorothy whispered. "I am positive that the end of the play has been altered so as to make a happy curtain. Go and see Mr. Harcourt, and ask him why he left out the scene that followed after the heroine sees the other girl with the necklace in her hand. Herbert Stirling may not have used that incident, but I feel absolutely sure that he did. It was too dramatic to be overlooked. It is a game of bluff you have to play."

German looked at his watch. Apparently he had come to a decision.

"I'll do it to night," he said. "Harcourt always spends half an hour at the Colly Cibber Club before he turns in. I'll go and catch him in the smoking room. It is just possible that our fascinating friend will fall into the trap. You go back home, my dear, and I'll let you know the result of the interview as soon as possible."

An hour or so later German strolled into the smoking room of the Cibber. The place was deserted save for Willoughby Harcourt and one other member. A little time afterwards the actor manager and the prominent theatrical agent were alone together.

"By the way," German said breezily, "I've got to congratulate you on another brilliant success. I've just seen Tuson, who ran up to Manchester to do the show for his paper. He gave me quite a vivid account of the story. Founded on fact, I am given to understand. But I fancy you made a mistake in cutting out the scene after the heroine sees the girl with the necklace in her hand."

Harcourt stood smilingly there; his vanity was soothed. His mind was full of his play; he could see nothing of the artfulness of the suggestion. He walked blindly into the trap.

"I had to cut it out," he said. "You see, it would have utterly spoilt my ending. If I had allowed it to stand, we must have finished on the tragic note. But what do you know about it?"

"Oh, we dramatic agents learn a few things," German said. "Don't forget that a good many plays come our way. Who is Eugene Malet? An assumed name, of course. A good many fools are going about saying that you wrote it. We know better than that—in fact, I know all about it. I came here to night to get Malet's address from you."

After all, the thing had been quite easy. And there was no drawing back for Willoughby Harcourt now. He looked just a little queer and white for the moment. He began to congratulate himself on the fact that he had not really claimed the authorship of the play. One glance at German's square jaw decided him. It would be better to speak out honestly.

"To tell you the truth," he said engagingly. "I am quite in the dark. The man came to me and asked me to read his play—he wrote me that he was tired of his life, that his story was there, and that he was going to put an end to it all. A paragraph I read in the paper a few days afterwards decided me that he had put an end of it. To make a long story short, I looked at the play and I liked it. The man was dead and buried, there was nothing to be gained by telling the story. Of course, I have laid no claim to be the author of the play, and if fools like to say so that is no business of mine. I'll send you Eugene Malet's letter if you like."

Mark German was quite content to let it go at that. A week later the popular society weekly called O.I.C. came out with the following paragraph:—

"Quite a romance (writes our esteemed correspondent, Mr. Mark German) attached to Willoughby Harcourt's latest and greatest success 'The Last Word.' The play is really the work of Mr. Herbert Stirling, at one time a promising writer of short stories. The heroine is inspired by a certain young lady to whom Mr. Stirling was at one time engaged, and from whom he was parted by a singular chain of most unfortunate circumstances. Mr. Stirling is somewhere abroad just at present, but if these lines should catch his eye he is asked to communicate with the above at 445, Craven Street, where letters are awaiting him."

"Miss Dorothy Nation, who is acting as secretary to Lady Mannington, tells me that the new song by that gifted composer is dedicated by permission to H.S.H. Princess Von der Zeidler. Lady Mannington intends to remain in Stratton Street till the end of the month."

"If he is alive that will fetch him," German chuckled as he read the two paragraphs which were artfully set side by side. "A man who can write a play like that doesn't commit suicide."

A week later, a visitor called at Stratton Street to see Miss Nation. She was quite alone in the drawing room as he came up. He did not say much; she said nothing at all. It was a very long time before either of them spoke. They had other things to occupy their attention.

"And now, my darling,"—Stirling broke the silence at length—"please tell me all about it. It reads like some wonderfully realistic stage play."

"It is a play," Dorothy laughed happily. "We'll write it together, if you like, dear, and we will get our friend Willoughby Harcourt to produce it."

CHAPTER V

THE MAN IN POSSESSION

That kind of thing is very amusing when it takes the form of a Christmas story in a theatrical paper; but to those who know, the element of tragedy is not lacking. There is no more light hearted and cheery soul than your Thespian, but he finds no real amusement in the knowledge that he is stranded, practically penniless, in a strange town where credit is impossible and he himself is more or less an object of suspicion. It requires a stout heart to face a poor landlady at the end of the first week with the information that her rent and the little odds and ends will not be forthcoming. It is harder still when there is a woman in the case.

There was nothing new in the situation—it had happened hundreds of times, and it will happen some hundreds of times more. Mr. Clarence Crawshoy, of the West End theatres, the darling of fashion and the admired of kings, had, in a fit of absent mindedness gone off on the Saturday evening with the week's exchequer, and there was no indication that he had the slightest intention of returning. That astounding fur coat, those darling white spats, and that brilliant (Alaska) diamond stud would awaken envy in the hearts of 'The Indian Girl' company no more. In other words, they had come 'up against' the inevitable provincial tour swindler, and most of them were penniless. It is all very well for Raymond Duke to tell the story now to his guests in Hill Street after coming home from his own theatre in London; but it was a very different Raymond Duke who crept along to the shabby little lodgings over the news shop in High Street, Marborough, to tell his pretty little wife what had happened.

"I felt sure that that man was a rascal," Netta Duke said.

"We all knew it," Duke groaned. "We knew it from the first. We felt it before we began to rehearse the show. Still, when one's been 'out' for ten weeks, anything is good enough to risk. The mischief is done, Netta. I've got ninepence and you have one and two. Mrs. Meekins's bill will be at least twenty five shillings. I wonder what she will say when I tell her."

It was no easy task. It never is an easy task for an honest, sensitive minded man to explain that he really is not a rascal, when all the time hard fact testifies to the contrary. Mrs. Meekin was distressed; she declared (with truth) that she had suffered like this before. She declared (also with truth) that theatricals had gone away vowing a cheque next Friday, and that, like the Good Samaritan, she had seen their face no more. She relaxed slightly, finally she wept and produced something charming in the way of supper, alleging (not with truth this time) that the good things had come as a present from her sister in the country. It was all very funny, very human, and very real.

'The Indian Girl' company met next day in conference. Something had to be done. They had played all the week to fairly good business, for Marborough is a thriving little place and trade was good. But for a lamentable weakness of Mr. Clarence Crawshoy in connection with the '3 o'clock race,' things might have been far more propitious. But that was all over now. Something had to be done. They were a mixed crowd, and a variety entertainment looked the proper course to adopt. The Mayor and many of the leading citizens were approached; by midday on Monday, Marborough had heard the story. And on the whole, Marborough behaved very well.

'The Indian Girl' company did not ask for much. They had a week's rent of the hall to pay, their landladies and laundresses to satisfy, and a further week's provisions to buy. If this could be cleared off and railway fares to London provided, all would be well. It sounded a modest programme enough, but it represented a capital sum of not far short of fifty pounds.

The benefit performance was fixed for Friday night. All being well, the company would leave for London the same evening somewhere about twelve o'clock. Enough money had been taken during the week to keep things going, and Friday was expected to wipe out the deficit altogether. There was every promise of a bumper house. It was late on the Friday afternoon that the sinister rumours began to go round. Confirmation came from Signor Biardi, the world renowned conjurer, who arrived in Marborough to attend a children's party in the evening.

"Lord bless you," he told Duke and some of the others. "What I couldn't tell you about Clarence Crawshoy isn't worth knowing. Bad egg from the start, dear boys! Been doing this kind of thing for years. Dealing with anybody but a crowd of professionals, he would have found himself in gaol long ago. Oh, there are no flies on Clarence Crawshoy!"

"But how can he possibly hurt us?" Duke asked.

"Easy as falling off a house, dear old chap," the Signor explained. "Crawshoy only skipped as far as Middlesborough. Saw him there yesterday. Trying to borrow the price of a brief to London. Good thing for you if he'd raised it. Because he knows what is going on here, and he's hatched a pretty little conspiracy to get his share of it. You see, in law, he is still responsible for the hall here; he owes a good bit for printing, and there is a judgment out against him on this account. He's got a little sweep of a printer in Middlesborough to buy up this debt for a sovereign or two, so that he stands your creditor. It's a goodish sum that is owing, and if this little man comes along about half past seven to night and takes possession of your box office, where are you? He can take every cent until his debt is paid, and that will just about clear you out. He'll come over with some County court official, and it will be too dangerous to defy him. Afterwards he will divide the swag with Crawshoy, and all will be well, as the melodrama says."

"Do you know this as an absolute fact?" Duke asked anxiously.

"I do," the Signor said solemnly; "I had a bit of printing done at the same shop, and the foreman, who is a decent sort, told me. Fact is, he asked me to give you a tip."

All this was pleasant hearing! A fair sum of money had resulted from the sale of tickets, but quite another was calculated as the takings at the door. Unless something in the nature of a miracle happened, love's labour would be lost. They debated the matter solemnly and seriously for the best part of an hour. The low comedian began to see his way.

"This is decidedly a case where strategy is required," he said. "It is no time for half measures. Signor Biardi, kindly favour me with some particulars of this creditor of ours. Tell me something as to his personal appearance and his characteristics. Is he an athlete?"

"Oh, Lord, no!" Biardi responded. "Anything but. A greasy, nervous little beggar—sort of a man who would do anything for money. The loss of it would arouse what little pluck he has. He isn't looking forward to coming here at all. He'll probably leave the County court bailiff at some eminent pub, and come personally to make a compromise. He'll be content with twenty pounds. And ready to make a 'sacrifice' to save anything in the way of unpleasantness."

"Webster, the 'low comedian merchant,' smiled. He was seeing his way quite clear now.

"The little blackguard shan't get a penny," he said. "Only leave it to me and we shall quit the place by the advertised train with all the swag in our pockets. We shall have time to pay everybody, and clear out at the cost of paint and a few feathers. Only the programme must be altered slightly. I am going to give an imitation of an Indian snake charmer. Miss Elaimi is lending me the tame pythons she uses in the title role of 'The Indian Girl.' My show was intended to be a burlesque, of course. As a matter of fact, the audience will be deprived of the opportunity of interviewing that masterpiece of humour. It is a thousand pities, but in the circumstances it can't possibly be helped. Duke, when the time comes, you will have to announce that, owing to a sudden indisposition, the snake charming scene will be omitted. See that the minion from the County court is tracked down to the pub, where, doubtless, he will be in waiting, and arrange for him to be placated with unlimited beer. This is only a precaution, but it will be just as well for us to take it. Rig up the little dressing room on the prompt side as an office, and when our little printer comes, see that he is shown into the office at once. 'On with the dance, let joy be unconfined,' and all that sort of thing. Pay everybody, say good bye, and look out for me at the last moment at the station. Meanwhile, advance me ten shillings."

"What for?" Duke asked prudently.

"Why, to save the situation, of course. As a matter of fact, I am going to buy half a dozen of those sand bags they used here in the winter time to keep the cold air from coming in between the window sashes. They are long bags in red flannel. If you want to know what they are required for, I shall decline to tell you. Let it be sufficient that they are intended to save the situation. The rest of the dark and bloody secret is mine."

And Webster refused to say any more. He departed armed with his half sovereign, and for the rest of the afternoon was conspicuous by his absence. Spies from the theatrical camp carefully watched the trains from Middlesborough, and just after half past six a message arrived to the effect that the force was in sight and was bearing down on the hall. Presently the rear guard called a halt at the Three Compasses, where he was speedily joined by an affable carpenter, who loudly proclaimed the fact that he had had a good day starting price betting, and was almost morbidly anxious that all and sundry should share his good fortune. In this way half the invading force was speedily, permanently disposed of—the conscientious carpenter had seen to that.

A shock head of black hair and a greasy face was thrust into the box office window, and a voice, intended to be firm, asked for Mr. Duke. The box keeper was politeness himself. He understood that Mr. Duke was down in his office checking the takings, and would the gentleman go and see him there? The gentleman in question intimated that he desired nothing better. All he wanted was his share of the plunder and to avoid anything like a personal explanation with the boys in the gallery. He began to take fresh heart of grace, and the large lump at the back of his throat was diminishing rapidly. An attendant ushered him into the office, and banging the door, hurried back to his duties.

A figure bent over the desk under the gaslight—a figure the like of which the little printer had never looked upon before. The figure rose to his full height and glanced at the intruder. His face was black as ink, his hair hung over it in long ringlets. His brow was surrounded by a great headdress of feathers that hung far behind. The dress on the whole reminded the printer of the literature of his boyhood. Here was the dusky Redskin of the plain, palpable and in the flesh. It was also palpable that he was exceedingly annoyed. He advanced with a threatening gesture.

"What is it the little white man desires?" he asked. "Why does he intrude upon us when our heart is turned towards the great Maker of the Universe? Why does he pollute the hour of meditation?"

"Take one," the Indian said hospitably, "take two, take the blooming. The dusky children of the forest are harmless!"

The printer stammered something to the effect that it was all a mistake. The Indian stalked solemnly across the room and locked the door. He appeared to be muttering incantations. Then, to the sweating horror of the printer, he plunged his brown arms into a basket on the table and produced a glittering, scaly, writhing mass of living snakes. They wriggled over the table.

"Take one," the Indian said hospitably. "Take two—take the blooming. The dusky children of the forest are harmless so long as my eye is on them. But don't move, don't so much as wink an eyelid, or you are lost. Folks say that I am mad. They lie in their beards. It is for a penance that I am doing this thing in your land of fogs and snow. The Great Spirit ordained it and I obey him. I yearn for no blood tonight, the desire for peace is upon me."

He advanced upon the timid printer and coiled two snakes about his neck. The intruder collapsed into a chair, the snakes writhed and wriggled on the floor. Then very carefully and solemnly, the Indian collected them into his basket again. With dry lips the printer essayed to speak.

"Silence," the Indian whispered. "The spirits are abroad and they will hear you. Even the snakes like like death in their presence. Behold, pale face, look for yourself!"

He took up the basket again and dragged from it a pile of those loathsome reptiles. He tossed them about the floor, by the door, along the skirting, where they lay absolutely still and motionless. To a terrified and distorted imagination they were snakes—they could be nothing else but snakes. All the same, they were nothing else but window bags filled with sand and procured at an outlay of some few shillings. But they served the purpose as if they had been so many cobras.

"Now let us understand that the spirit is upon us," the Indian said solemnly. "Do not move until I return, as you value your safety. Anon, paleface, I will join thee again. Bit if you move... I will turn down the gas—ah, have I already warned thee of thy fate, rash man?"

The printer uttered no further protest. He sat there in the dark, listening to the noise and bustle outside; he heard the clock strike the hour of eleven. He became aware of the fact that the silence was getting more and more oppressive. The clock struck twelve, the hoot of a distant railway whistle told him that the last train for London was starting, but he did not connect that fact in any way with his imprisonment. That confounded Indian had forgotten all about him, of course. And he sat there with his feet drawn up, trembling and sweating in the knowledge that death in a score of hideous, creeping shapes was all around him. Finally, he fell into a weary slumber, and there the daylight found him, cold and uncomfortable, but not forgotten.

"The beggar swallowed it like milk," the low comedian explained, amidst shouts of laughter, as the train proceeded towards London. "Never saw such a state of funk in your life. Only shows you what imagination will do even for the most practical of us."

CHAPTER VI

A PAIR OF HANDCUFFS

It was quite a new departure for so high class a crowd as the Sutton Vascombe Opera Company, but from the financial point of view it had been a great success. The company were on sharing terms, though the general public was not supposed to know that. The expenses had been heavy, and something had to be done. More than half the chorus were dismissed, two thirds of the orchestra found engagements in Melbourne or Sydney, and then 'the grand tour' of the 'back blocks' began. It was somewhat rough and ready, but the miners and sheep shearers did not mind that. They got the best of singing and acting for their money, which they put down freely. There were mining villages where the exchange was pure dust—an ounce for a stall, and in proportion for the gallery, so that the exchequer was actually getting heavy with gold that had yet to see the mint. The treasurer was naturally a little anxious—it was a wild district, and 'robbery under arms' was not yet altogether a thing of the past. Jim Baynham came that way sometimes, and when he did somebody had to suffer. Jim was the last word in the way of bushrangers—an Englishman who had left his country for his country's good; there were warrants out for his apprehension in England. For the last five years he had been ever the delight and terror of the territory between the Poonah and the Yarra. He was by way of being a gentleman, too, and he could do the thing very well when he chose. On the other hand, he could behave with the most cold and malignant cruelty.

Consequently the secretary of the Sutton Vascombe Company was uneasy in his mind. He was responsible for some twelve hundred ounces of gold dust, and there was no chance of conveying it to a place of safety. He confided his fears to all and sundry. They treated him lightly—they had no fear of Jim Baynham. The women were nervous, of course—Marjorie Hickson, for instance. She was a sweet little girl with a sweet voice, and she was going far in her profession. Meanwhile, she had a brother just recovering from a serious illness, and lying in a Melbourne hospital, who was entirely dependent upon her for the time being. And in turn he had a wife in England. If anything happened to Marjorie's share of the treasury, she trembled for the consequences.

"None of 'em care," the treasurer groaned. "Seem to think that actors are exempt from troubles of that kind. They say that Jim Baynham was in the house at Banawaddy. Just as if that was going to make any difference. And that chap Claxton agrees with me. He knows the ropes. Been out here for years, he tells me."

Claxton had joined the company at Paira River. He was understood to be the surviving actor of a variety company which had been utterly stranded a year ago. Claxton had been down with fever, and when he was on his feet again, it was only to stand in his last pair of boots with the last shilling in his pocket. He had drifted up against the Sutton Vascombe combination just at the time when they were short of an assistant baggage man. The mere fact that Claxton was undoubtedly a gentleman weighed very little with the company. The knowledge that the stranger had been in vaudeville was enough. They never even asked him what his line was. Most of them had been recruited from the Universities, a good many of the women bore good names. They really were a 'tony' crowd. They admitted that the baggage man was a gentleman; therefore they tolerated him. But, artistically, they made him aware of the awful gulf between them.

With the sweet unreasonableness of her sex, Marjorie took to Claxton from the first. She was sorry for him—she felt sure that he had been the victim of misfortune. She admired his square, handsome face, and that well knit figure of his. His eye was clear, his check was brown—he could not have passed anything but a clean, wholesome existence. He had been all over the world, too, and had many an interesting story to tell. At least, Marjorie thought them interesting. And whenever her mind wandered uneasily in the direction of bushrangers, she was curiously confronted by the knowledge that Claxton was travelling with the company.

He was a little man, with a clean cut, alive face, with a great beak of a nose all on one side: a mass of thick black hair was brushed back from the forehead and fell over the nape of his neck. A thin, clean shaven mouth was parted in a smile that disclosed a really splendid set of teeth. He was dressed in a neat, double breasted, blue serge suit; his brown shoes shone with a glittering polish. In his right hand he had a revolver.

They had played for two nights near Sendigo when the drama began in earnest. People had come from far and near to see the show—they were prepared to travel home under the coolness of the stars, and the village was deserted. The so called 'hotel' was filled with the company, to the exclusion of everybody else; supper was a thing of the past, and the management had retired. Most of the combination were still in the big pitch pine dining room, talking over the events of the evening, when the door was suddenly pushed open and a stranger entered. He was a little man, with a clean cut, alive face, with a great beak of a nose all on one side; a mass of thick black hair was brushed back from the forehead and fell over the nape of his neck. A thin, clean shaven mouth was parted in a smile that disclosed a really splendid set of teeth. He was dressed in a neat, double breasted, blue serge suit; his blown shoes shone with a glittering polish. In his right hand he held a revolver.

"Mr. James Baynham, greatly at your service," he said gently. "It is as well, perhaps, to remark that the first suggestion of resistance on the part of any of you gentleman will result in a vacancy in the company. I should deeply deplore this, as I am a musician myself. To shoot a tenor or precipitate a baritone into an untimely grave would be a source of lasting sorrow to me."

Nobody moved for a moment. They were taken utterly by surprise, there was not a revolver amongst the whole crowd; indeed it is doubtful whether a single member of the company had the slightest idea how to handle one. Marjorie Hickson crept a little closer to Claxton.

"Is that really the man, or is it somebody playing a trick on us?" she asked.

"Oh, that's the man right enough," Claxton replied. "We are old acquaintances. As a matter of fact, I was at school with him in England."

"Oh, indeed! And is he really quite as bad as people—"

"Worse," Claxton said curtly. "He's a born rascal. As a matter of fact, he couldn't be anything else. Some chaps are like that, you know. We shall have to make the best of it."

Baynham was speaking again. He was understood to say that he was not alone. He had come with two other intimate friends of his for a little music. The friends were engaged at that moment taking precautions against a surprise on the part of the hotel management. He regretted that he would be compelled to take similar measures so far as the male members of the company were concerned. There were too many of them for safety; they boasted too many athletes.

"We raided the police station at Garralong as we came here," Baynham said smilingly. "It was necessary to my scheme that we should have some handcuffs. We found some score of pairs, and they are at present in the bar. Very sorry, of course, but the thing must be done. You gentlemen will kindly line up against the wall, facing it. Ladies, we are your devoted slaves. No harm shall come to any of you. Now, you chaps!"

The last word rang out like a threat. Claxton shut his teeth together grimly.

"It might be a great deal worse," he whispered to Marjorie. "You will see where I come in presently. Don't worry about your share of the exchequer, and don't be afraid. No harm will come to any of you girls. You will have to sing and play until they have had enough of it. We shall look on with our hands fastened behind our backs. It's a grim joke, but you will see presently that there are two sides to it."

Marjorie smiled bravely. She heard Baynham utter a curse as Caxton lagged behind. He strode up to Claxton and caught him by the shoulder. Then he started back.

"Good evening, James," Claxton said mockingly. "Quite an unexpected pleasure, isn't it? Never expected to see me again. Nice sort of life you are leading, isn't it? Wonder how a family like yours managed to turn out such a waster! It would have been far better if we had let you down that day in the Monk's Pool below Chesham Bridge."

Baynham's lips parted in a snarl.

"So it's Claxton," he said, "Claxton of the Sixth. Head of the school. The shining example to the rest of us! Kicking about Australia juggling, or something of that kind. Very glad to meet you again, Phil Claxton. I shall know how to deal with you presently. Be so good as to point out the treasurer of this powerful operatic cast to me. He is suffering from over anxiety, and I want to relieve him of some of it. Oh, yes; the little man in the spectacles. Still, pleasure before business is always my motto. Where is the music? I expect the piano is a sufficiently ancient instrument, but we must make the best of that. Now, ladies, please."

Two other men came trooping into the room at the same time. There was nothing in their appearance to give cause for alarm. They were neatly and quietly dressed like their chief, and were openly amused at the sight of the helpless row of men facing the wall.

"Have you got the bracelets there?" Baynham asked.

The glittering pile of handcuffs were produced and handed to the leader of the raid. One by one he fitted them on the wrists of the male members of the company. The quick snapping of the locks was the only sound that could be heard.

"So far so good," Bayham said cheerfully; "I am sorry that you will not be able to smoke, gentlemen, but you can stand there with your hands behind you and listen to the concert. When it is over I shall be able to relieve the anxious mind of your treasurer, and after that I will place the key of the handcuffs on the old green tree where the roads cross about a mile away."

The concert began promptly. The performers were palpably nervous, but that wore off after a time. At any rate there was no violence to be feared. They might lose all their money, but there was ample time to make some more. And, after all, the situation was not devoid of comedy. The light heartedness of the artistic nature was asserting itself. Marjorie Hickson had sung a song that had been received by the select audience with singular favour. Claxton stood with a group of men about him whispering something in their ears. They seemed to be interested in what he was saying. Claxton had a chance to say a few words to Marjorie presently.

"I am very thirsty," she exclaimed. "It is such a hot night. Please get me some lemonade."

Baynham turned to his colleagues. They hurried off in the direction of the bar. Claxton strolled across the room towards Baynham. There was an ugly gleam in his eye. Baynham saw it and rose to his feet instinctively. Instantaneously his hand went to his hip pocket. Then he smiled as if half ashamed of himself. Claxton's hands were securely fastened behind him. Nothing but a miracle.... the miracle happened. Claxton's right fist appeared with the left end of the handcuff dangling from it. The heavy metal described a gleaming circle in the air, then it came down with a sickening blow on the parting of Baynham's thick black hair. Something spurted hot and red as Baynham pitched headlong to the floor and laid there lost to all creation. The thing was so startling, so dramatic, so utterly unexpected, that no cry came from the ring of white faced women looking on. Claxton flung himself on the prostate body and hastily searched Baynham's pocket. He held up something not unlike the key of an ordinary beer barrel.

"Gather round," he said hoarsely. "Stand in a group as naturally as you can. I can release two or three of you if you will be quick. Make a stage scene of it—nobody should be able to do it better."

Baynham's subordinates came bustling into the room carrying glasses and bottles. As they advanced somebody stumbled against one of them, and a glass smashed on the floor. There was a scramble to pick it up, and an instant later the two outlaws lay at the bottom of a veritable football scrimmage. The thing was done almost without a word being spoken.

"I think that will about do," Claxton said, after the discomfited ruffians had been searched. "Take this key, somebody, and release the rest of the crowd. I don't know who you two rascals are, but I expect the police do, and that comes to the same thing. I've laid open the head of your chief, and he is not likely to do any more mischief for some time to come. Now let's release the landlord and the hotel staff and get them to ride for the police."

Claxton's popularity was assured now. The story spread like wildfire all through the colony. Baynham was safe in jail with his followers; he was never likely to do any more mischief. The whole thing was a piece of coolness and courage calculated to appeal to the Colonial mind. But nobody quite knew how Claxton had managed to get rid of his shackles. He did not in the least seem disposed to talk about it either. It was Marjorie Hickson in whom he finally confided.

"It was quite easy," he said. "I'll tell you, because you are the only one who has been really nice to me. Besides, I'm giving up the game and going home. My uncle is dead, and I have come into his property. As a matter of fact, the whole business was a piece of wonderful good luck. These chaps here wanted to know what my line was, and I refused to say. I was a Handcuff King. I learnt the dodge from a professor in England. I have a wonderful pair of wrists, and I can get out of anything. When these handcuffs were produced by Baynham, I saw my way at once. He might just as well have tied me up with a piece of cobweb. I waited till he felt quite comfortable, and then I took him unawares, as you saw. You'll keep my secret, Miss Marjorie."

Marjorie thanked him with tears in her eyes.

"You have saved everything," she said. "I don't know what I should have done without my money. I was going to offer to share it with you, but since you have so much—"

"Then let me share with you," Claxton said eagerly. "I shall never enjoy it alone. And the worst of the thing is, there is such a lot of it, my dear. I hope you are not offended."

But Marjorie was not in the least offended. She was not even annoyed when Claxton kissed her. And she has seen no reason to repent her decision since.

FRED M WHITE – A CONCISE BIBLIOGRAPHY

NOVELS (A-Z)

Ambition's Slave (1916)
The Argus Eye (1919)

Blackmail (1902)

The Blue Daffodil (1934)

The Brand Of Silence (1911)

A Broken Memory (1929)

The Bubble Reputation (1908)

By Order Of The League (1886)

The Cardinal Moth aka The Accused Orchid (1903)

The Case For the Crown (1918)

Claxton's Mill (1912)

A Clue In Wax (1930)

The Corner House (1905)

The Councillors of Falconhoe (1922)

Craven Fortune (1904)

A Crime On Canvas (1909)

The Crimson Blind (US title: The Mystery Of The Crimson Blind) (1905)

A Daughter Of Israel (1892)

The Day: Or The Passing Of A Throne (1914)

A Deal In Letters (1923)

The Devil's Advocate (1924)

Dropped From The Fast Express, or A Daughter's Sacrifice (1911)

The Edge Of The Sword (1907)

The Ends Of Justice (1906)

A Fatal Dose (aka Behind the Mask) (1907)

The Fight For The Child (1925)

The Five Knots (1907)

"Found Dead" (1930)

The Four Fingers (US title: The Mystery Of The Four Fingers) (1907)

A Front Of Brass (1910)

The Garden O' Dreams (1909)

A Golden Argosy (1886)

The Golden Bat (1924)

The Golden Rose (1909)

The Green Bungalow (1923)

The Grey Woman (aka Sinister House) (1928)

The Happy Exile (1920)

A Harbour Of Refuge (1918)

Hard Pressed (1910)

The Honour Of His House (1920)

The House Of Mammon (1913)

A House Of Sorrows (1911)

The House Of The Schemers (1906)

The House On The River (1925)

In Trust (1892)

Jim Crowshaw's Mary (1911)

The King Diamond (1927)

Lady Clara (1913)

Lady Edna's Awakening (1920)

The Lady In Blue (1915)

The Law Of The Land (1906)
The Leopard's Spots (1920)
The Lonely Bride (aka The White Bride) (1907)
The Lord Of The Manor (1907)
Love, The Foe (1910)
A Maker of Millions (1909)
The Man Called Gilray (1911)
The Man Who Found Christmas (a novelette) (1915)
The Man Who Knew (1932)
The Man Who Was Two (1921)
The Man With The Vandyk Beard (1925)
The Midnight Guest: A Detective Story (1907)
A Mummer's Throne (1910)
My Lady Bountiful (1905)
The Mystery Of Crocksands (1923)
The Mystery Of The Ravenspurs (aka The Black Valley) (1911)
The Mystery Of Room 75 (1922)
Naboth's Vineyard (1889)
The Nether Millstone (1906)
Netta, The Story Of Sin (1909)
New Century Calendar Clue (1948)
Number Thirteen (1914)
The Old Secretaire: A Christmas Story (novelette) (1887)
On The Night Express (1930)
The Open Door (1907)
Paul Quentin (1908)
Paul, The Sage (1910)
The Phantom Car (1929)
Powers Of Darkness (1912)
The Price Of Silence (1925)
The Psalm Stone (1905)
Queen Of Hearts (1930)
A Queen Of The Stage (1908)
The Riddle Of The Rail (1926)
The Robe Of Lucifer (1896)
A Royal Wrong (1913)
The Salt Of The Earth (1918)
The Scales Of Justice (1908)
Secret Of The River (1934)
The Secret Of The Sands (1911)
A Secret Service (1913)
The Seed Of Empire (1916)
The Sentence Of The Court (1913)
A Shadowed Love (1905)
The Shadow Of The Dead Hand (1926)
The Silver Stream (novelette)
The Slave Of Silence (1906)
A Society Jezebel (1917)

The Sundial (1908)
Tregarthen's Wife: A Cornish Story (1901)
The Turn Of The Tide (1923)
The Weight Of The Crown (1904)
The White Battalions (1900)
The White Bride (aka The Lonely Bride) (1910)
The White Glove (1910)
The Wings Of Victory (1919)
The Yellow Face (1906)

SHORT FICTION SERIES

THE MASTER CRIMINAL (1897-1898)

A series of 12 short stories featuring Felix Gryde, who describes himself as "a really clever soldier of fortune."

The Head Of The Caesars
At Windsor
The Silverpool Cup
The "Morrison Raid" Indemnity
Cleopatra's Robe
The Rosy Cross
The Death Of The President
The Cradlestone Oil Mills
Redburn Castle
"Crysoline Limited"
The Loss Of The "Eastern Empress"
General Marcos

THE LAST OF THE BORGIAS (1898)

A series of stories featuring Professor Victor Colonna, a vigilante physician who murders undesirable people with undetectable poisons.

The Scrip of Death
The Crimson Streak
The Holy Rose
The Saving Of Serena
The Varteg Necklace
The Three Carnations

DRENTON DENN - SPECIAL COMMISSIONER

Drenton Denn is a tough newspaper reporter on the payroll of The New York Post. His hallmarks are a straw hat, a Norfolk jacket, a perennial cigar, and a terrier by the name of "Prince."

The Yellow Moth
The Red Speck
Dust
The Fire Bugs
The Great White Moth

THE ROMANCE OF THE SECRET SERVICE FUND (1900)

This series features Newton Moore, the top agent at The Secret Service Fund.

By Woman's Wit
The Mazaroff Rifle
In The Express
The Almedi Concession
The Other Side Of The Chess Board
Three Of Them

THE DOOM OF LONDON

This sci-fi series of six stories describes a variety of catastrophes which ravage London.

The Four White Days
The Four Days' Night
The Dust Of Death
A Bubble Burst
The Invisible Force
The River Of Death

THE SAGE OF TYBURN (1905-1906)

Each of these stories was preceded by the header The Sage Of Tyburn.

No. 1 - The Chronicle Of The Yellow Girl
No. 2 - The Chronicle Of The Blue-Eyed Syndicate
No. 3 - The Chronicle Of The Inconsequent Princess
No. 4 - The Chronicle Of The Elderly Adonis
No. 5 - The Chronicle Of The Libelled Velasquez

THE DRAGON-FLY (1909)

Six stories about an impecunious but brilliant amateur criminologist, entomologist and ornithologist by the name of Horace Daimler. Each of the stories was preceded by the header The Dragon-Fly.

No. 1 - How Horace Daimler Got His Name
No. 2 - The Three Red Rats
No. 3 - [title unknown]
No. 4 - [title unknown]
No. 5 - A [illegible] Crime
No. 6 - The Mirror Over The Fireplace

REAL DRAMA (1909)

A series of stories published under the subtitle "Being Some Leaves From The Notebook Of A Late Theatrical Agent."

His Second Self
An Extra Turn
"Not In The Bill"
The Plagiarist
The Man In Possession
A Pair Of Handcuffs

THE TELEPHONE STAR (1912)

A series of stories about Keith Marrit, a star journalist working for a fictitious newspaper called The Telephone.

No. 1 - The Case Of El Hamid, The Seer
No. 2 - The Case Of The Genuine Counterfeit
No. 3 - The Case Of The Yellow Car
No. 4 - The Case Of Lord Wintercotte
No. 5 - The Case Of The Rusty Nail
No. 6 - The Case Of The One-Eyed Chauffeur

GIPSY TALES (1903-1916)

A series of stories describing the adventures of a wily British navvy with Romany roots, who is known only as "Gipsy." In his fantasies Gipsy portrays himself as a playwright, and tries to stage-manage the dramatis personae and the situations that feature in the stories.

A Matter Of Kindness
A Liberal Education
A Stranger In Bohemia
Drops Of Water

The Unpremeditated Curtain
Mere Details
Out Of Season

THE DIARY OF A LONELY SOUL (1915)

The Diary Of A Lonely Soul - Story 1 [title unknown]
The Diary Of A Lonely Soul - Story 2 [title unknown]
The Diary Of A Lonely Soul - Story 3 [title unknown]
The Diary Of A Lonely Soul - Story 4 [title unknown]
The Diary Of A Lonely Soul - Story 5 [title unknown]

AN A-Z OF OTHER SHORT FICTION

According To The Statute
The Ace Of Hearts
Adventure (aka A Trick of Fate)
After Reynolds
Alias "James Jones"
An Ally
And This Is Fame
Anonymous
The Apple-Green Plate
Applied Mechanics
The Arms Of Chance
Art Critics
At Short Notice
Aunt Mary
Autumn Manoeuvres
The Azoff Diamonds
A Bad Cold
The Balance Of Nature
The Barrister At Bay
Below Zero
The Better Way
Big Fish
The Big Thing
Billy's Xmas
A Bit Of Egypt
The Black Admiral
The Black Cat
The Black Narcissus
The Black Prince
Blind

Blind Chance
The Blindworm
A Block Of Marble
A Bootless Errand
Brayton's Secret
The Broken Lute
A Broken Sceptre
The Broken Trail
The Buff Gauntlet
Burglar Bill's Pupil
By Grace Of His Majesty
By Wireless
A Call On The Phone
A Captious Critic
The Case For The Prisoner
The Charlatan
A Christmas Bride
A Christmas Deputy
Christmas Cards
The Christmas Carol
A Christmas in Peril
A Christmas Star
The Clock Struck Twelve
The Colonel's Christmas Pudding
Compounding A Felony
The Convict
Coralie And The Pearls
A Corner In Elephants
The Courage Of Despair
Crossed Swords
The Dancing Shadow
The Daughters Of The Moon
A Daughter Of Nature
The Dawnstar
A Deal In Diamonds
Denny
A Derelict In Clover
The Desert Ship
A Dog's Life
The Doll's House
The Dormer Window
A Dose Of Quinine
The Doubting D, or, A Cranky Cryptogram
A Draught Of Life
Early Closing Day
An Eastern Princess
The Eavesdropper
The Ebbing Tide

The Egg Of The Little Auk
The Emsdam Dispatches
The Empty House
An Error Of Judgment
The Evidence For The Prisoner
Excess Profits
An Eye For An Eye
The Eye Of The Camera
The First Stone
The Foil
Forget-Me-Not
For Love's Sake
For Once In A Way
For Value Received
A Foster-Father
Found!
The Fourth Man
Free Labour
A Friendly Call
From Information Received
Full Fathoms Deep
Gabrielle
A Gamble In Love
A Game Of Draughts
A Garden Of Pearls
Gentlemen Of The Jury
The Gates Of Ramshi
The Grey Bat
The Grey Raider
The Guiding Star
The Half-Crown Princess
The Hand Invisible
Hardy's Big Coup
The Heart Of The Anarchist
Heavy Metal
The Heels Of The Dawn
Her Christmas Dawn
His Christmas Gift
His Majesty's Mails
A Hole In The Net
The Hospitallers
Ice In June: A Playwright's Story
Icky Of Oluk Lake
Imperial Preference
In Black And White
In Rosemary Lane
In The Dark
In The Fog

In The Pit
Introducing Mr. Pentsymon
The Joinville Tunnel
Judgment Reserved
Karma
Kindergarten
The Kingmaker's Token
Lady Mary's Bulldog
The Language Of Flowers
The Last Drive
The Law Of The Jungle: A Tale Of Mean Streets
The Leather-Pushin' Private
The Left Hand
The Lesson The Ants Taught
The Livery Of Death
The Lonely Furrow
The Long Arm Of Bronze
Love In Aether
The Luck Of The Game
Made In England
The Man Himself
The Man Who Got Through
The Man Who Rang The Bell
The Man With The Eyeglass
A Masked Battery
The Master's Voice
A Matter Of Habit
'Merica
A Message from the Flood
The Midnight Call
The Missing Blade
The Missing Note
The Mistletoe Bough
Moray The Traitor
More Than Coronets
The Morning Glory
Music Hath Charms
A Musical Treat
The Mystery Of Room Five
Natural Selection
Nerves
The Night Express: The Story Of A Bank Robbery
The Northern Light
Not On The Records
An Object Lesson
The Odds On Zero
One Day With A Working Ant
One Foggy Night

One Of The Old Guard
On Peace Night
The Onus Of The Charge
The Orpheusia
Ostentation
The Other Man's Story
The Pardon
A Parrot Cry
The Path Of Progress
The Pawn And The Rook
Pearls Of Price
Photo By Lesterre
Pictures In The Snow (a Christmas story)
A Place In The Sun
The Platinum Chain
A Popular Novelist
Poste Restante
A Prize Crop
Proof Positive
The Purple Terror
A Queen In Hiding
A Question Of Money
Rachel's Seventh Year
Rawhide Science
The Real Dramatic Touch
A Record Round
Red Petals
Rob Peter—Pay Paul
A Rope Of Snow
Rose Of The Desert
A Royal Bag
The Royal Train
The Salmon Poachers
Santa Anna
A Satisfactory Reference
Saviour From The North
The Second Chapter
Second In The Field
The Shebeeners
A Single Hair
Sir Jeremiah's Big Shoot
Sister Louise
The Sixteenth Chapter
A Sleeping Partner
Sleeping Partner
A Sound In The Night
"Special" To The Telephone
A Stolen Interview

The Straight Game
The Stranger Within The Gate
Sub Rosa
The Substitute
The Superman
The Supreme Test
The Sword Of Justice
A Table Tragedy
The Thirty-Seventh Month
This Little World
A Thrilling Exit
The Throat Of The Wolf
The Ticket
To Be Let Furnished
Treasures Three
The Two Bon-Bons
Two Of Them
The Unbelieving Eye
Unbidden Guests
The Unexpected
An Unrecorded Crime
The Vital Spark
The Vital Spot
War Ribbons
The Waterwitch
The Western Way
When The Moon Set
The White Geranium
The White Spot
White Wings (1922)
The Wings Of Chance (1922)
The Witness (1920)
The World Next Door (1916)

www.ingramcontent.com/pod-product-compliance
Lightning Source LLC
Chambersburg PA
CBHW061505170626
46811CB00004B/1616